The Great Adventures of
Piggy the Peruvian Pig

THE GREAT ADVENTURE OF
PIGGY
THE PERUVIAN GUINEA PIG

NEW YORK

The Great Adventures of Piggy the Peruvian Pig

© 2016 Sarah King.

Published in New York, New York, by Morgan James Publishing. Morgan James and The Entrepreneurial Publisher are trademarks of Morgan James, LLC. www.MorganJamesPublishing.com

The Morgan James Speakers Group can bring authors to your live event. For more information or to book an event visit The Morgan James Speakers Group at www.TheMorganJamesSpeakersGroup.com.

ISBN 9781630475680 paperback
ISBN 9781630475703 eBook
ISBN 9781630475697 hardcover
Library of Congress Control Number: 2015902155

Shelfie

A **free** eBook edition is available with the purchase of this print book.

CLEARLY PRINT YOUR NAME ABOVE IN UPPER CASE

Instructions to claim your free eBook edition:
1. Download the Shelfie app for Android or iOS
2. Write your name in **UPPER CASE** above
3. Use the Shelfie app to submit a photo
4. Download your eBook to any device

Cover and Interior Layout by:
Chris Treccani
www.3dogdesign.net

Illustrated by:
Sarah King

In an effort to support local communities, raise awareness and funds, Morgan James Publishing donates a percentage of all book sales for the life of each book to Habitat for Humanity Peninsula and Greater Williamsburg.

Get involved today, visit
www.MorganJamesBuilds.com

Habitat for Humanity®
Peninsula and
Greater Williamsbur
Building Partner

To Catie,
who loves all creatures great and small.

And to Chris, the boldest and bravest man I know.

PRAYER
"Hear and bless thy beasts and singing birds, and guard
with tenderness small things that have no words."

This is the great adventure of Piggy the Peruvian Guinea Pig. Piggy and his girl, Catie, played together in the garden. Catie called him bold and brave as he ventured forth, searching for ever more tender grasses in the great outdoors. One afternoon while they were out with Catie's friend Erin, Piggy saw a clearing where the yummiest green grass was growing. He had to go and try it.

That green grass was delicious! He ate and ate.
It was so yummy, he wanted to share it with his
friends. Piggy looked up, but Catie and Erin had
disappeared! Where was his garden? He squeaked
and bweeped for Catie.

In the garden, Catie and Erin searched and called. Where had Piggy gone?
Catie searched for him until it was too dark out to continue.

Piggy's squeaks brought Owl over, hungry for his dinner. He ran as fast as he could into the forest. He did not feel bold and brave now. He missed his girl.

That night Catie watched out her window for him. Would Piggy be bold and brave? Would he be afraid of the dark?

Piggy *was* afraid of the dark. He listened to the night noises and waited for the morning sun. The roots of a tree became his nest. He tried to be bold and brave.

Finally the sun came up and Piggy set
out to find his girl. He came across
Fawn lying in the grass. Fawn had
never seen a guinea pig before.

"I have lost my girl, Catie," said Piggy. "Have you seen her?"

"No," said Fawn. " You should ask Rabbit and Mouse."

Piggy found Rabbit and Mouse eating lunch. "Have you seen a little girl named Catie? She is my girl and I lost her in the garden yesterday."

"Sorry, no," said Mouse.

"We haven't seen her," said Rabbit. "You should try Turtle. He lives by the pond."

As Piggy left he heard Mouse say to Rabbit, "Do you think he stayed out all night by himself? That Piggy must be bold and brave."

Piggy felt a bit better.

"Hello Turtle, have you seen a little girl named Catie? I lost her yesterday while we were playing in the garden."

"Nope," said Turtle. "No one comes here much because of the…"

"Ssssnakessss?" Out of the tall grass suddenly slithered Snake.

"Come clossser," said Snake. "I don't know where the girl is, but I do know sssssssomething…"

"What is that?" asked Piggy.

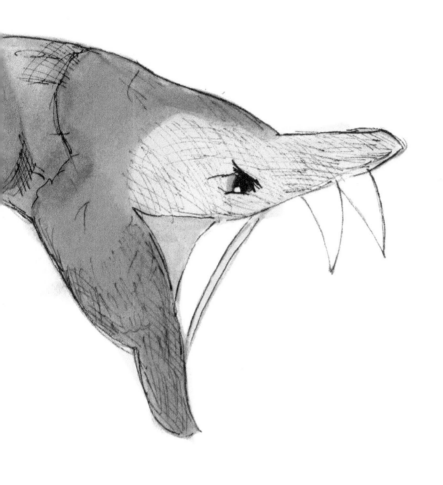

"I HAVE FOUND MY LUNCH!"

Piggy puffed himself out and jumped up and down, chattering his teeth.

"I am NOT snake lunch! I am Piggy the Bold and Brave!"

"Sssshhheessh," said the surprised Snake. "You'll be too tough to ssswallow."

Piggy scurried down a nearby path. He came across a house, where a puppy was playing with a ball.

"Excuse me," said Piggy. "Have you seen my girl Catie? I lost her yesterday in the garden."

"You smell familiar, who are you anyway?" asked the puppy, Leo.

"I am Piggy the Bold and Brave, who has outrun Owl, scared Snake, and traveled a long way. But I still can't find my home," Piggy sniffled.

"My you *are* bold and brave. Wait here, I will go get my girl.

She is in the house playing with her friend. Maybe she can help."

Piggy hid under the porch and waited. Soon he heard barking and a familiar voice. He squeaked and bweeped as loud as he could and the voice got closer.

"What is the sound, Leo? I think its coming from under the porch." Erin looked down, and Piggy bweeped happily. He ran towards his friend.

"Catie, Catie!" she called. "Come look!"

Laughing and crying tears of joy, Catie swept Piggy up into her arms.

"How did you get all the way out here?" Catie said. "What a bold and brave boy you are!"

Piggy squeaked happily. He had found his girl. He was home.

Author's Note

Sarah King is an artist working in many mediums. She lives in New York City with her husband Sean, and their puppy, Leo. She grew up inside the Mannassas Battlefield Park in Virginia. This is a true story about her cousin's guinea pig. Piggy was lost for three weeks in the park before being returned safely by neighbors.

Special thanks to the MALS Program at Hollins University, particularly Ruth Sanderson, whose wisdom and guidance brought this book to life. I would also like to thank my family and friends for their encouragement and lots of coffee! Thanks especially to the people at Morgan James, who made this book a possibility. And to Piggy, who let me tell the story of his first great adventure.